Snakes Are Nothing to Sneeze At

Gabrielle Charbonnet

Snakes Are Nothing to Sneeze At

Illustrated by Abby Carter

A Redfeather Book

Henry Holt and Company · New York

Text copyright © 1990 by Gabrielle Charbonnet
Illustrations copyright © 1990 by Abby Carter
All rights reserved, including the right to reproduced
this book or portions thereof in any form.
Published by Henry Holt and Company, Inc.,
115 West 18th Street, New York, New York 10011.
Published in Canada by Fitzhenry & Whiteside Limited,
195 Allstate Parkway, Markham, Ontario L3R 4T8.

Library of Congress Cataloging-in-Publication Data
Charbonnet, Gabrielle.
Snakes are nothing to sneeze at / Gabrielle Charbonnet;
illustrated by Abby Carter.
(A Redfeather book)
Summary: Although he's not furry and her best friend thinks he's
yucky, Annabel loves her new pet snake.
ISBN 0-8050-1373-3
[1. Snakes as pets—Fiction.   2. Pets—Fiction.]   I. Carter,
Abby, ill.   II. Title.   III. Series.
PZ7.C   1990
[E]—dc20   89-26919

Henry Holt books are available at special discounts
for bulk purchases for sales promotions, premiums,
fund-raising, or educational use. Special editions
or book excerpts can also be created to specification.

For details contact:

Special Sales Director
Henry Holt and Company, Inc.
115 West 18th Street
New York, New York 10011

First Edition
Designed by Victoria Hartman
Printed in the United States of America
1   3   5   7   9   10   8   6   4   2

For my mother and father
—G.C.

And for my mother and father also
—A.C.

Contents

1

Easy for You to Say

"Sit, Brandy, sit!" said Annabel, pushing down on Brandy's back end.

"Silly!" Charlotte laughed. "You can't make a dog sit in *water!*"

Annabel and Charlotte had been busy all morning getting Charlotte's golden retriever, Brandy, ready for a dog show. Charlotte's father had put Brandy in the bathtub, and the two girls began to wash him with special dog shampoo.

"Here," said Charlotte, "you sort of hold him down while I try to—"

Annabel put her arms around Brandy's neck while Charlotte rinsed him off with the shower hose. Although she was as sopping wet and soapy as Brandy was, Annabel didn't mind. She wished she had a dog as nice as Brandy.

"Ugh. I think he's all rinsed off now," said Charlotte. She looked down at her soaked clothes. "This is the worst part. I hate getting all messy."

"What do we do now?" asked Annabel.

"Daddy will come get him out for us," Charlotte said, and went to the door to call her father.

Charlotte's father helped Brandy jump out of the tub so Charlotte and Annabel could start drying him off with old beach towels.

"Thanks, Daddy. We're okay now," Charlotte said.

"There, there. Good dog," said Annabel, nudging Brandy into the middle of the bath mat.

"Here." Charlotte handed Annabel a soft dog brush. "You do the front half, I'll do the back."

"This is so fun," Annabel said as she started to fluff and dry Brandy's chest and legs. "It's like playing beauty parlor, only better."

Charlotte smiled. "Well, it's not that fun after you've done it a million times. I'm tired of being covered with dog hair."

Still, Annabel noticed that Charlotte looked like she was enjoying fluffing Brandy's tail so it stood in a perfect curve.

"You're such a good boy, aren't you, Brandy?" said Annabel, smoothing the soft hair on his head. Brandy glanced at her with a pained look in his brown velvet eyes. Charlotte laughed.

"He's not being *good*, he's being bummed out! He hates this!"

"Nooo, he doesn't hate this. Do you, Bran— Oh!"

Suddenly Brandy's nerves snapped, and he leapt out of

reach, leaving girls, brushes, and towels behind him. In a dash for freedom, he galloped toward the staircase. He paused at the top to give himself a good shake all over.

"Oh, no! Daddy, help! Brandy's escaped!" Charlotte looked at Annabel in despair. "*Do* something! The last time he did this he went and rolled in the dirt!"

Brandy gave himself a good final shake and looked back at the girls as if to say, "Don't take this personally."

But his moment of hesitation was enough for Annabel. "Wait, I'll catch him!" she yelled, and leapt forward in the flying tackle her little brother used on her all the time.

"And he's down! The crowd cheers!" Annabel expertly pinned Brandy to the ground. Charlotte's father arrived in time to help Annabel up, then he and the girls pushed a reluctant Brandy toward the bathroom for a major refluffing.

Brandy was subdued, and didn't try to escape again. The girls determinedly picked up their grooming brushes.

"What happens at a dog show?" asked Annabel, gently smoothing Brandy's soft ears.

"Well, it's kind of boring, actually. Daddy walks Brandy around in a circle with a bunch of other dogs, then he walks Brandy by himself, then Brandy runs around once by himself, and finally they stand in the center of the ring while the judges look Brandy over and pick up his tail."

"Are there lots of other dogs?"

"Yes," Charlotte replied, buffing Brandy's toenails. "All

sorts of dogs—some of them are really funny looking. And they all have these long names that no one could ever remember."

"It sounds like fun," said Annabel.

"It's fun the first time. After that it gets dull. But my dad does it because the more times Brandy wins, the more people will want their dogs to have puppies with Brandy. They pay Daddy a fee to use Brandy."

Annabel was shocked. She was crushed that there was a *business* reason behind all this. She had thought that Charlotte's dad did it just because he was proud of Brandy.

All the same, Annabel wished she could go with Charlotte to a dog show sometime.

Today, however, she had to go home because her aunt was coming over for dinner, so she gave Brandy one last stroke from tip to tail and kissed his square, silky head to wish him luck.

"Bye," said Charlotte. "I wish you could come."

"Me too," said Annabel. "Call me later and tell me how it went."

"Okay."

Annabel walked home dejectedly. Charlotte was so lucky to have Brandy. Annabel didn't have *anything*. When Annabel got to her house, she went into the backyard and sat on the back steps, her chin in her hands. She could hear her little brother, Michael, playing ball out front.

If only Michael were a sister and not a stinky boy, she thought. If I had a sister, I wouldn't need a pet. Annabel's father was allergic to dogs and cats. They made him sneeze. Also guinea pigs, hamsters, bunnies, and parakeets. And horses. When the family went to visit Uncle Pat's farm, her father had to stay inside in the air conditioning and blow his nose.

It wasn't fair having a father who was allergic to everything. Everything *fun*.

"Annabel, dinnertime!" her mother called. Annabel went inside. They were having pork chops and sweet potatoes, which Annabel liked.

After dinner, Annabel's father asked Annabel to turn off the sprinkler in the backyard. "And would you please coil the hose up again?"

"Okay," said Annabel. "I'll be right back."

"Thanks," her father said. He was washing dishes with his blue rubber gloves on.

Annabel went into the backyard. It was almost dark outside. She turned off the water spigot and began pulling the hose into a pile. When she reached down to start coiling it, she thought she saw the grass move. She blinked and looked closer. It *did* move! Then Annabel saw two small, shiny eyes. It was a snake! A little green snake!

"Oh!" Annabel jumped back.

The snake froze.

"A snake!" whispered Annabel. "A real snake!" She tried to decide whether to touch it or not, but while she was thinking, the snake made a dash for it and disappeared into the grapevines on the fence.

Annabel quickly finished putting the hose away and walked back to the house.

A real snake! she thought.

The next day Annabel looked for the snake. She looked in the bushes and under the trees, and she lay on the grass and ran her fingers through it. But she didn't see him.

She looked up *snake* in the encyclopedia. She found a picture that looked exactly like hers. It was called green grass snake.

"Yup, he's green all right—but it's not a very exciting name," Annabel said to herself. "If I catch him, I'll call him Wilfred." Wilfred was a lovely name.

According to the picture, her snake was almost full grown. The encyclopedia also said that his typical diet was spiders, insects, and earthworms. Bleah. *But* they had no fur, unlike cats, dogs, hamsters, and horses. And bunnies. They did have teeth, but they were very small, not like fangs. And grass snakes weren't at all poisonous.

That night, Annabel called Charlotte to see how Brandy had done in yesterday's dog show.

"Not bad," said Charlotte. "He got Best of Breed, but Best

in Show went to a dog from Belgium with a name I can't even pronounce."

"Oh, too bad. But I bet Brandy *looked* the best."

Charlotte giggled.

Annabel was torn—should she tell Charlotte about her plans for a pet of her own? "Listen, Charlotte," Annabel said, "what do you think of snakes?"

"I think they're yucky and slimy," Charlotte said.

"Oh. What if a snake was the only pet you could have?" Annabel asked.

"Then I guess I wouldn't have a pet," Charlotte answered.

Easy for you to say, thought Annabel, when you have a golden retriever at home.

Days went by and Annabel didn't see Wilfred again. But just in case, she made a little home for him out of an old aquarium she found in the garage. She washed it out and dried it with paper towels. There was a crack in one side, but Annabel carefully sealed it with masking tape. She put some of her mother's gardening sand in the bottom and planted a clump of grass in the sand. Next she got an old blue bowl and piled sand around the edges so that when it had water in it, it looked like a little forest pool. With some smooth rocks for decoration and a small branch to climb on, it was perfect.

Still no Wilfred.

Then one day she was playing ball with Michael in the

backyard. Michael wasn't the best pitcher in the world, and Annabel wasn't the best catcher. They spent a lot of time running after the ball and picking it up.

Michael threw the ball hard and it hit a tree, then bounced over Annabel's head and rolled underneath the azalea bushes. Annabel ran after it and poked her head under the bushes to find it. But guess what she found instead?

2

~~~~~

Not Slimy at All

It was Wilfred.

Without even thinking, Annabel shot out her hand and grabbed Wilfred around his middle. Wilfred started to wiggle. Annabel almost dropped him and held him as closely as she could without squishing him. She pulled him out from beneath the bushes very slowly.

"What's that?" asked Michael. "Oh, yuck, it's a snake! Is it alive?"

"Yes," said Annabel. "He's *my* snake. His name is Wilfred." Wilfred had stopped wiggling and was turning his head around, trying to look at Annabel.

"Come on, Wilfred," she said, and headed for the garage.

Michael followed her as she pulled the prepared aquarium out from where she had hidden it.

"Who's Wilfred?" he asked. "Where did you get him?"

"This is Wilfred," Annabel said, putting the snake inside

the aquarium. "I got him just now in the garden." Wilfred lay draped over his climbing branch and didn't move. Annabel and Michael peered over the edge and watched him. Still he didn't move.

"You scared him," said Annabel. "Move back."

"What are you going to do with him?" whispered Michael.

"I'm going to keep him," said Annabel. "He's going to be my pet."

"What will Mom and Dad say?" Michael was still whispering, and watching the motionless Wilfred.

"They aren't going to find out," Annabel replied firmly. She turned to look hard at Michael. "*Are* they?"

"Well, I guess not," said Michael.

They sat and watched Wilfred for a while, but even Annabel got bored after almost ten whole minutes of Wilfred's not moving an inch.

"How do you know it's a him?" Michael asked.

Annabel thought for a moment. The encyclopedia had drawings to show the difference between a male snake and a female. Annabel couldn't tell the pictures apart.

"Well," she said finally, "if he has babies, he's a her. But until then, he's a him."

"Oh. What do snakes eat?" he asked.

Ah. *This* she knew.

"They eat insects and spiders and earthworms," said Annabel. "Maybe he's hungry, and that's why he's not moving. He's not dead, because I see him breathing. I'll go get him something to eat."

Annabel covered the top of Wilfred's aquarium with a piece of heavy plywood, then pushed the aquarium back against the wall and threw an old camping tent over it, as though the tent had just fallen there by itself.

"I want to stay and watch," said Michael.

"No. You can't see Wilfred when I'm not here," said Annabel. "He's *my* snake, and I don't want you touching him."

"Yuck, who would want to touch a slimy old snake!" Michael snorted. "I just want to look at him."

"He's not slimy," said Annabel, going back to the house with Michael following. "He's sort of smooth and soft and cool. Not slimy at all."

In the kitchen Annabel found an old mayonnaise jar with a lid. She got a nail and a hammer and punched holes in the top of the jar.

"What's that, honey?" her mother asked, coming into the kitchen.

"Just a jar. I'm going to catch spiders in it," Annabel said truthfully.

"Oh, well, just no bugs in the house, okay?"

"Okay, Mom."

Once the jar was ready, Annabel went upstairs. In the back

of the guest room, there was a small door that led from a closet into the attic. Annabel got her father's flashlight from beside his bed and crept through the door. The attic wasn't a fun attic, with wonderful old trunks full of neat clothes that you could play dress-up with. It was mostly just filthy, and had piles of old school papers and a hat stand and some incredibly ugly lamps that looked like lumps of orange concrete. There were a few broken chairs, nothing worth fixing up, and an old dressmaker's dummy that Annabel played with for a while, turning the knobs to see how big she wanted her chest to be when she grew up. And of course there were . . . spiders. And plenty of 'em.

Annabel poked around under the eaves with the flashlight, and when the light shone on a spiderweb, she moved in closer and looked for signs of activity. A few webs were empty, but then she hit the jackpot and captured spider after spider. If they were in the web, she rounded them up by twisting their webs on an old knitting needle. If they were in midair, she just moved her finger through the strand so that it stuck to her, and then she lowered the spider into the jar by its own spinner thread. Soon she had six spiders of various sizes.

I hope Wilfred likes this kind, she thought as she screwed the lid on tight.

Back in the garage, she uncovered the aquarium and pulled it out. Wilfred had moved! He had coiled himself up in a

corner, with the end of his tail hanging in the blue bowl of water.

"Here you go, boy," Annabel said, and emptied her jar over the aquarium, using her knitting needle to dislodge the sticky spiders. They fell in a webby tumble over Wilfred's climbing branch and started scrambling away. One large spider (the fattest, Annabel noticed) was hanging by a thread from the climbing branch, spinning anxiously toward the ground. Wilfred spotted it! He looked interested!

Annabel held her breath as Wilfred very, very slowly started to uncoil. It looked like his middle moved all by itself and his head and tail stayed put. Finally, she saw his little green head inching closer to the dangling spider. He shot forward. Snap! Annabel almost fell backward and felt the tiniest bit scared. She leaned toward the aquarium again. The big fat spider was gone. Wilfred was perfectly still. Then Annabel saw him swallow. She had two feelings: Success!—and— Bleah! All those crawly little legs going down his throat! Ugh! She was very glad that he had decided to have a little some-thing, but she didn't know if she could watch him eat any more spiders.

"Annabel! Dinnertime!" her mother called from the back door. Annabel's stomach felt a little queasy. She didn't really feel like having any dinner. She looked at Wilfred, who seemed to be hunting around for another snack. Annabel decided he could go after the rest by himself. She put the plywood on top of the aquarium.

"Bye, Wilfred. I'll come back tomorrow. I hope you enjoy your spiders," she added. Then she covered him up with the old tent and walked back to the house.

She couldn't believe she finally had a pet of her very own. He was hers. She had found him herself and was taking care of him. In the back of her mind she worried about keeping a secret from her parents, but she had no choice—was there any way they would let her have a snake for a pet?

3

First Spiders, Now Worms!

Annabel visited Wilfred every day after school. Some days Charlotte came over to play, and then Annabel had to wait until after dinner. Annabel remembered what Charlotte had said about snakes, and knew she couldn't share the secret of Wilfred with her. It was the first time she could remember *not* telling Charlotte something.

One day Charlotte came over, and they went into Annabel's backyard.

"Boy, it's almost summer. That will be so great," said Charlotte.

"I can't wait." Annabel sighed. "No more homework! No more wearing dresses! Just play, play, play, all day long."

"No more stinky Barry Johnson, always pulling my hair," said Charlotte with feeling.

"Oh, I know," said Annabel. "He's the worst. Think of

how awful it would be if you were his mother, stuck with him forever." Charlotte laughed.

"Yuck-o!" she said. "Or marooned on a desert island!"

"Aiieeee!" Annabel screamed, laughing.

The two girls lay on their backs in the cool green grass and looked at the sky. There was nothing better than lazing around and knowing that every second that ticked by was one less second until school was out.

"Actually," said Annabel thoughtfully. "Actually, if you *had* to be stuck on a desert island with someone, who would it be?"

"Hmmm," said Charlotte. "Besides you, you mean?"

"Yeah. Like if it had to be a boy. A boy from our class. And you were stuck with him forever on an island somewhere. For the rest of your life."

"Oh, gross! From our class?" Charlotte chewed on the end of her hair while she thought. Her nose wrinkled. "Oh, gol, forever? I don't know. The whole idea is disgusting. Anyway, who would you pick?"

"I don't know. Maybe I would pick Wilfred," Annabel said quietly.

"Wilfred? We don't have any Wilfreds in our class."

"Oh, I know," Annabel said airily. "I just like the name."

"I don't know any Wilfred," said Charlotte. She stared at Annabel. Annabel looked down and picked some grass. How could she tell her best friend, who thought snakes were yucky and slimy, that she had one hidden under an old tent only twenty feet away?

After Charlotte left, Annabel had a few minutes before dinner. She headed for the garage. Gradually, Wilfred had been letting Annabel touch him gently without his freezing into a statue. Now she leaned her head against the edge of the aquarium and stroked his smooth skin. Maybe he wasn't as cuddly as a puppy or kitten, she thought, but he *was* very sweet.

Wilfred moved over his new climbing branch. Annabel had replaced the old one with this one, which was a little bigger and more complicated for him to play on.

She could feel his little ribs as he glided over the branch, his black tongue darting out as he made his way up to the top of the aquarium. Annabel heard footsteps—but it sounded like Michael.

"Annabel?" he called softly.

"In here, Michael. It's okay."

Michael came in and knelt next to her on the cool cement floor. "How's he doing?" he asked.

"He's fine, but I'm running out of spiders fast. I have to switch to worms."

"I know. I saw the holes along the fence. Why don't you wait until it rains? Then you could just go pick them up off the sidewalk."

"I can't wait that long, dumbo. Wilfred will be hungry before then—won't you, boy?" she said, and rubbed his green head, which he bravely permitted.

Gathering worms was not as easy as spiders. For one thing, they were much grosser, and Annabel wouldn't touch them with her hands. She had to loop them over a stick, and they always fell off a couple of times before she got them in her jar. On the other hand, one worm kept Wilfred happy for much longer than even five or six spiders. When Wilfred ate just one worm, the hungry look faded from his eyes for several days.

That night after dinner Annabel had to go worm hunting. Her mother was working in her office, Dad was washing the dishes, and Michael was watching TV, which he wasn't allowed to do, as it was a school night. Annabel figured that she had at least half an hour to herself.

The places along the fence were still wormless. She decided to try around the trees in the backyard, but no luck there, either. The ground was too dry. All the worms had gone farther underground, looking for water.

The back door swung shut. It was Annabel's father. He was walking toward the garage!

"Dad!" Annabel called, to divert him. He saw her in the dusky light and came over.

"Hi, kiddo. What are you doing out here? Why have you been making little holes everywhere?"

"I'm looking for worms," Annabel said.

"First spiders, now worms!" he said.

Oh, no. Mom told him about the spiders, Annabel thought. How was she going to explain *that?*

"What do you need worms for? Going fishing?" He smiled.

"Uh, they're for a class project. About insects," Annabel lied. She had to. It was to protect Wilfred.

"But neither worms nor spiders are insects," her father pointed out.

"Oh. Oh, right, I mean, it's about 'Things You Can Find in Your Backyard,' " Annabel stammered.

Her father laughed. "Well, how about 'Things You Can Find in Your Garage'?" he asked. "I need some paint." He headed back toward the garage.

"Dad! Wait!" Annabel was desperate. Her father was sure to notice the aquarium. But maybe not. Maybe he would just get the paint and not find Wilfred at all. In which case she would just give everything away by acting weird.

"What is it, honey?"

"Oh, nothing," Annabel said. "Just thought I'd come with you." Casual, act casual.

Inside the garage, Annabel's father shone his flashlight on the cans of paint lining the shelves.

"I need . . . um . . . Manor White," he murmured. Annabel stood next to him, her hands clasped behind her back, trying not to look at Wilfred's tent.

"Ah! There it is!" Her father reached up and pulled an old paint can off a shelf. He blew the dust off it.

"Manor White! Great!" Annabel let out a silent breath of relief and turned to leave.

"Now all I need is a paint cloth. This will be perfect!" Annabel spun around just in time to see him yank the old tent off Wilfred's aquarium.

Annabel gasped in horror, but her dad didn't seem to notice. Wilfred's plywood clattered to the ground. Annabel's father reached down to pick it up, and Wilfred, happy to have someone visit him, poked his head out to say hello—right in her father's face.

Her dad actually yelped. He yelped and jumped back a step. This scared Wilfred, who pulled back quickly into the safety of his aquarium. Annabel's father's eyes followed him and saw the aquarium pushed against the wall.

"What *is* this?" he asked. He pulled the aquarium out and peered into it with his flashlight. There, curled up in a corner, staring straight ahead, was Wilfred, in all his bright green glory.

Annabel knew she was in big trouble, but she couldn't help admiring the way the beam of light reflected off his smooth skin.

"This is a snake," Annabel's father said. "This is a grass snake in an aquarium in my garage." Annabel couldn't argue, of course. For a moment she wondered wildly if she should

deny knowing anything about him ("Maybe a stranger put him there—"), but then she looked at Wilfred's proud little head and knew she simply couldn't.

"Whose is this? What is this doing here? Is this Michael's?" her father asked.

Annabel swallowed. "That's . . . that's Wilfred," she said in a small voice.

4

Can I Keep Him?

"Wilfred?" her father said. "Is this yours? Do you know about this?" Annabel looked at the ground. What if her dad made her get rid of Wilfred? She had tried not to think about it before. Now she felt like she might cry.

"He's my . . . he's my Wilfred. My pet. My pet snake."

"Your pet *snake*? When did you get a pet snake?"

Just then Annabel's mother came out to look for them. She found them by the open garage door, with Annabel rubbing her eyes and Annabel's father kneeling by the aquarium.

"A snake! Where on earth did that come from?" Annabel's mother asked. That did it—Annabel burst into tears.

"He's mine! He's my pet! He's the only pet I can have!" she sobbed.

Annabel's mother and father looked at each other. Annabel's mother pulled her closer and let Annabel hide her face in her sweater. She stroked Annabel's hair.

"There, there," Annabel's mother said. "Why don't you tell us about your snake?"

Annabel kept sniffling, but she told them about helping Charlotte groom Brandy and wanting a pet of her own. And then seeing Wilfred the first time, and fixing up the old aquarium, and finding him suddenly under the azalea bushes.

"Is this why you've been digging up my garden?" her mother asked. Annabel nodded.

"And why you were catching spiders in the attic?" her father asked. Annabel nodded.

"How long have you had this snake?" her mother asked.

"His name is Wilfred. Almost a month." Annabel sniffled some more.

"A month! And what were you planning to do with Wilfred?" asked her father.

"I was going to keep him!" Annabel burst into tears all over again. Her parents looked at each other some more.

Then Annabel's mother said, "Is Wilfred a grass snake?" Annabel nodded.

"He eats spiders and worms? And what else?" her father asked.

"Almost any kind of insect," Annabel said.

"Does he bite?" her mother asked.

"No. Not my Wilfred. He only has baby teeth," said Annabel.

"And he stays in this aquarium all the time?" her mother asked.

"Yes," Annabel said, "except when I take him out to play with him. Then I put him back."

"Well, John, what do you think?" Annabel's mother said. Annabel couldn't believe it. Were they really thinking about letting her keep Wilfred? That would be so great!

"Well, if he doesn't bite and isn't poisonous, and he eats only insects—I suppose it could be worse. He isn't going to shred the furniture, he doesn't need to be taken for walks—"

"He doesn't bark," said Annabel, interrupting him.

"He doesn't shed fur," said her mother.

"He won't bite the mailman," said Annabel's father, laughing.

"He can be our guard snake!" said Annabel.

They were laughing and looking down at Wilfred. Michael came out to see what the commotion was, and he was happy that Wilfred could stay.

"That's great!" Michael said. "Is he going to stay out here in the garage?" Everyone quit laughing. Annabel looked hopefully at her parents.

"Could he . . . could he stay in my room? I promise he'll never, ever get out. I'll take good care of him, you'll never have to see him at all, I promise. Cross my heart and hope to die," Annabel pleaded, and crossed her heart. "And he won't be nearly as much trouble as a dog or a cat," she added, to sort of remind her father that it was really his fault that she had a snake at all, because of his allergies.

It worked.

"Well, if it's okay with your mother, it's okay with me," he said uncomfortably.

"Well, I guess it's okay with me if it's okay with your father," her mother said. "I guess."

"Yay! Hooray! Hooray for Wilfred!" yelled Annabel and Michael, jumping up and down.

5

Friends Don't Have Secrets

Now that Wilfred was no longer in hiding, Annabel had no choice but to show him to Charlotte.

"Oh, a snake! Isn't he yucky?" Charlotte asked, wrinkling her nose. Annabel wanted to cover Wilfred's ears so he couldn't hear. But she didn't think she could find his ears, even if she looked.

"He isn't at all yucky. He's really nice. Why don't you pet him and see?" Annabel said.

"Oh, no way!" shrieked Charlotte, so loudly that Annabel was sure it hurt Wilfred's hearing. Annabel didn't make her pet him, but she thought Charlotte was being silly and kind of a sissy. Anyone just looking at Wilfred could see that he wasn't yucky at all. Even Michael said so now.

"Anyway, when did you get him?" asked Charlotte.

"I found him almost a month ago and he's been living in the garage," Annabel said.

"You *found* him? You found him and you just picked him up?" Charlotte asked incredulously.

"Yes. I knew he wasn't poisonous. I didn't tell you right away because you said you thought snakes were yucky and slimy," Annabel said.

"You had him a *month* and didn't tell me about it?"

"I thought you wouldn't like him," Annabel explained.

"Well, Annabel, if I had something that you thought was yucky and I knew that you thought it was yucky but I still had it, I would *tell* you that I had this yucky thing. Even so," Charlotte said.

Annabel looked down. Maybe she *should* have told Charlotte right away—but . . .

"I'm sorry," said Annabel. "He just had to be a secret for a while. Because of my parents."

"Friends don't have secrets, Annabel Bentley," said Charlotte. She looked at her watch. "I think I have to get home for dinner," she said, and turned to go.

Annabel looked at her clock. It was four-thirty.

That weekend, Annabel's father made a better top for Wilfred's aquarium. Instead of the old piece of plywood, Wilfred now had a nice screened top that let in light and air. He seemed to like it. Annabel put him on top of her bookcase in her room in front of the window, so he could look out if he wanted to.

Every afternoon when Annabel came home from school, Wilfred was there for her, either sleeping in the sunshine or coiling himself around his climbing branch, looking for something to eat. Once or twice he was even pushing his little head against the new lid as though he was ready to play.

Annabel's father took her down to Murray's Bait 'n' Tackle Shop, and they bought boxes of mealworms and bait crickets. It was much easier to make Wilfred's dinner now that she didn't have to hunt for earthworms and spiders.

According to the encyclopedia, Wilfred was just about full-grown. Annabel put him on her bed and measured him with her mother's cloth measuring tape. He was just over twenty-six inches long. The biggest that green grass snakes ever got was about thirty-two inches long. Mostly they stayed around two feet or so. Still, with his regular and high-quality diet (everything at Murray's was strictly fresh) Annabel was hoping that Wilfred would continue to grow.

She made a growth chart for him out of an old roll of wallpaper. She wrote WILFRED'S GROWTH CHART at the top of it in big green letters. Then she marked off three feet in inches, all along the bottom of the roll. She wrote the date of his last measurement right after the twenty-six-inch mark. She would measure him once a month and mark it down.

The next time Charlotte came over, Annabel showed her Wilfred's new lid and his growth chart. Maybe if Charlotte felt more included, she would like Wilfred better. But Charlotte didn't seem too interested in how long Wilfred was.

"Could we go play outside?" she asked.

"Sure. I'll bring Wilfred," said Annabel.

"Oh, I really don't want to play with your snake. He sort of gives me the creeps. Let's leave him in here, okay?" asked Charlotte.

Annabel felt miffed. How selfish of Charlotte. Annabel never minded if her stinky old dog wanted to follow them around, and said so.

"Annabel, it's hardly the same thing! Brandy is a nice, furry, cuddly dog! Wilfred is a snake!"

Geez, Annabel thought, it's not like he has *cooties.*

"Wilfred might not be furry, but he's my pet and I love him," Annabel said coolly. "If you don't want to play with my pet, fine, but don't expect me to play with yours. And quit talking about Wilfred in front of him. It hurts his feelings."

Charlotte rolled her eyes. "Okay, I won't talk about him. Let's just go outside," she said.

"Fine," said Annabel.

"Fine," said Charlotte.

They went outside and played, but it wasn't much fun.

For her end-of-the-year science project, Annabel wrote a report about Wilfred. She researched snakes some more at the

library and drew a snake family tree showing the different branches. She showed where Wilfred was on the tree, how he was of the colubrid snake family, and who his relatives were. She made a clay model of the inside of a snake, showing his digestion and lungs (long and skinny) and his little snake heart. And she took Wilfred to school in a special cloth snake bag that she had bought at Petworld. It had a drawstring top, and though she had to be careful not to mash him, it was much easier than lugging around his whole aquarium.

All the kids loved Wilfred. Annabel took him out of the bag, and at first he was shy in front of all the people. But he soon loosened up and twined happily around Annabel's shoulders, his tongue darting out as he went. Annabel let everyone pet him but not hold him, because she didn't want anyone to squeeze him too tight.

She got an A on her project, and she was the most popular girl in school that day, because of Wilfred.

6

A New Home for Wilfred

Almost before Annabel knew it, it was summertime, and school was out.

"Yay!" Annabel and Michael shouted as they raced home that last day. "Free, free at last!"

There was nothing better than summer vacation. After a couple of weeks, summer camp would start, and they would go swimming every day and do gymnastics. But first, Annabel had a mission: She wanted a better aquarium for Wilfred.

She went to Petworld and saw how much an aquarium the size she wanted would cost. Then she asked her parents for an advance on her allowance.

"Honey, if I give you that much of an advance, you won't get any more allowance until you're thirty," her mother said. Annabel's face fell.

"I really want to get Wilfred a better aquarium," she said. "There's a crack in the one he has now."

Annabel's mother asked how much a new one would cost, and Annabel told her.

"Hmm," said Annabel's mother. "That's a lot of money. But I have an idea. There are a lot of things around the house that your father and I don't have time to do. If you did them, we would pay you. And you could save up your pay to buy a new home for Wilfred."

"Okay. I think I could do that," said Annabel happily. "I want to start right away."

So Annabel and her parents worked out a job list. She would be paid by the job, and some jobs paid more than others. Hard or dirty jobs paid the most.

Annabel started the next day, weeding the garden. It was hot outside, and she got sticky and grimy. Her back felt like it was going to break. When she went inside to get some ice water, Michael said, "You look like the creature from the Black Lagoon."

"Shut up."

That night after her bath, Annabel got her dad's clippers and cut off all her fingernails because she couldn't scrub the dirt out from underneath. But it was all for Wilfred.

Charlotte called the next day and asked Annabel if she wanted to take Brandy to the park with her.

"Gee, Charlotte, I wish I could, but I have to do some chores around here," Annabel said.

"Can't you get out of them?" asked Charlotte.

"I guess, but I'm doing them to earn money. I want to get a new aquarium for Wilfred."

"Oh. Oh, well. Call me if you want to do something sometime," said Charlotte.

"Okey-dokey," said Annabel, and hung up.

In the days that followed, Annabel checked off jobs one by one. She:

✓) folded everyone's laundry
✓) cleaned out and organized the kitchen drawers
✓) Windexed the glass in the picture frames (didn't pay much, but it was inside)
✓) washed the car (and vacuumed it)
✓) washed *all* the downstairs windows outside (paid a lot because it was awful)
✓) cleaned the bathroom
✓) cleaned the refrigerator, inside and out (and found some disgusting stuff)
✓) washed the front steps
✓) trimmed the bushes along the side of the house

The day before day camp started, Annabel sat on her bed and counted up all the money she had been saving in her

bank. She smoothed out the dollar bills and put them in a pile. Then she piled up the quarters. (She had to make two stacks.) She didn't have many dimes or nickels, but she counted them carefully. She had enough! That night after dinner, her mother drove her to Petworld and Annabel bought a brand-new, shiny, perfect aquarium. And she had some change left over.

At home her father helped her take the aquarium out of the box and set it up.

"It's wonderful!" Annabel said. "Wilfred is going to love it—won't you, boy? You'll have so much room to move around!"

"You worked very hard for this," her father said. Then he turned to look at Wilfred sternly. "I just hope you appreciate what your mother did for you, young man," he told Wilfred, and Annabel laughed.

Camp started, and every morning Michael and Annabel caught the bus that took them across town. Annabel wished Charlotte went to day camp too, but she couldn't because she always went to her grandmother's for two weeks in the summer.

Wilfred had actually grown almost half an inch, and Annabel marked it down on his chart. She wasn't sure if he had really grown that much or if he had grown more than that, because it was hard to measure him. He wiggled. And he hardly ever stayed still when he was out of his aquarium—he was always off to see new places. But Annabel thought he had grown half an inch, and she felt very proud. She was taking good care of her pet.

7

An Uninvited Guest

One Sunday, when Charlotte had been at her grandmother's for a week, it was Annabel's mother's turn to have her literary group over for coffee. Once a month she got together with some people and they sat around and read poetry and stories.

The whole family was put to work cleaning the house. Annabel had to dust (even the tops of the picture frames) and her father had to cut the grass.

"Honey," he said to Annabel's mother, "are you sure they're going to notice the grass? Aren't they just going to go straight into the house?"

"I want the yard to look neat," Annabel's mother said. "For once, I want everything to look nice and neat."

It could be worse, Annabel thought. She could be like this all the time.

Poor Michael had to polish the silver coffeepot that was only used for special occasions. All morning her mother had been washing serving plates and opening cans of black olives and salted peanuts. Annabel cut up celery and carrot sticks and arranged them neatly in a circle on a platter. Her mother made a dip out of dry soup mix. It tasted great.

"Okay, now, don't eat all the dip," Annabel's mother said. "Leave some for the guests."

"Who's coming this time?" Annabel asked.

Her mother pushed a strand of hair off her face.

"Well, let me see. There's eight . . . no, nine. . . . Well, there's Mr. Peabody, there's Sarah Talbot, Tom Wallis the playwright, Mrs. Daphne Blue . . ."

"Daphne Blue?" Annabel asked. "What a funny name."

Her mother smiled. "Yes, and you know what—her favorite color really is blue. She always wears blue. Could you go check on your father, please? I want to make sure he's done before they get here."

Annabel went and checked on her father (he was almost done) and then went to her room. She leaned against her bookcase and looked out the window. She could see her father wiping his forehead outside. She was glad she had escaped before he asked her to help rake.

"Aren't you glad *you* don't have to cut the grass, Wilfred?" Annabel asked, looking down at him—only there was no him.

There was no Wilfred in his aquarium, and the screen cover was pushed off a little.

"Wilfred! Oh, geezum, where's Wilfred?" Annabel glanced around her room quickly, looking for a flash of green in motion—but no Wilfred. If Michael had taken him without permission . . .

But Michael was lying on his bed reading a comic book, recovering from the silver-polishing episode. He had not taken Wilfred out of his aquarium.

Would her mother have taken him for any reason? Maybe to show off to her literary people? Annabel was halfway to the living room when she realized that was a stupid idea. Her mother would never have taken Wilfred. Where could he be? The doorbell rang. The first guest was arriving. Annabel went back in her room and closed the door. She would go meet whoever it was later. First things first.

She looked under her bed and carefully felt underneath her bedspread and pillows. She looked behind the books in the bookcase. She checked the aquarium again. She shook out all the shoes on the floor of her closet. She went through everything on her desk. She picked up some dirty clothes on the floor. No sign of him.

With a sinking feeling, Annabel remembered Wilfred bumping his head against the lid. She had thought that meant he wanted to play and had taken him out. Now it looked as though he had let himself out and gone off somewhere. At least there were no other pets in the house to hurt him. Then Annabel had three bad thoughts:

1. Her parents would kill her if they knew that Wilfred had let himself out and was lost.
2. What if he had somehow gotten outside and was gone forever? (She couldn't think about that—it was too horrible.)
3. The house was full of strangers who didn't know Wilfred. They might step on him or something.

It was the "or something" that Annabel was really worried about.

Well, he wasn't anywhere in her room. He wasn't in the hall. He didn't seem to be in her parents' room. She heard her dad in the shower and hoped Wilfred wasn't in the bathroom. She went back to Michael's room. No Wilfred there—Michael helped her look. Annabel swore Michael to secrecy. No one must know that Wilfred had escaped.

"Annabel, honey, I'd like you to come meet some people," her mother called. Annabel swallowed hard and told Michael to keep looking, but to be inconspicuous.

Annabel went into the living room. It was full. She met three poets, one playwright, one essayist (whatever that was), one plain author, one teacher, and Mrs. Daphne Blue, who, as it turned out, wrote murder mysteries.

"They're incredibly gory," a poet whispered to Annabel.

"Why don't you sit down and have a cookie?" Annabel's mother suggested. "Mr. Peabody is our essayist. He's about to read for us." Annabel would much rather have been looking for Wilfred, but there was no way out. She smiled a weak smile and sat down. She quickly scanned the floor. No Wilfred.

Mr. Peabody was a small man in a brown suit. He was bald and had a brown mustache. He wore wire-rimmed glasses and seemed twitchy.

"Please, God, don't let Mr. Peabody find Wilfred," Annabel pleaded silently.

Mr. Peabody cleared his throat.

"I would like to read a short selection of my latest article, which I recently sold to *Gardens and More* magazine. It is entitled, 'My Favorite African Violet, and Why,' by Charles Peabody."

So that's what essayists are, thought Annabel—they write about flowers.

Mr. Peabody started to read. Annabel looked around. People seemed to be shifting in their seats. Annabel wondered if they really enjoyed these things or if they just put up with them. She ate another cookie. Then she took a piece of celery and dipped it in the dip. At her first bite, everyone turned, and Mr. Peabody looked over his essay at her. She quit chewing and swallowed hard.

Mr. Peabody was reading forever. Once Michael walked past the door and caught Annabel's eye. He shrugged his shoulders, then snuck away.

Finally Mr. Peabody finished. Annabel breathed a sigh of relief. People clapped politely, but they all looked relieved too.

Just as Annabel was preparing to slip out of the room, Mrs. Daphne Blue stood up and announced the title of her latest mystery.

"I call this *Death for Dessert*, by Daphne Blue." Annabel sank down into her chair again.

Mrs. Daphne Blue started to read. *Death for Dessert* was more interesting than Mr. Peabody's flower essay but still took far too long to get to the point, in Annabel's opinion. Annabel sat politely and watched the feathers on Mrs. Blue's hat bob up and down as she read.

Suddenly Annabel's eye was caught by a slight movement on the floor behind Mrs. Blue's feet. She watched in fascinated horror as a little green head slowly emerged from the air-conditioning grate on the floor.

Wilfred! How could he have gotten *there*? Annabel bit her lip and quickly looked around. No one else seemed to have noticed him. Yet.

Wilfred slithered further into the room as Mrs. Blue droned on. Annabel's heart was pounding. On the one hand, she desperately wanted Wilfred to sink back into the grate before anyone noticed him—and on the other, she thought, if he did, she might *never* find him again.

"Please, Wilfred, hide under the couch," Annabel prayed.

But Wilfred, after a cautious look around and a bit of tongue flicking, headed for the open doorway. Annabel stared at him, willing him to change direction.

Just then, Mrs. Daphne Blue reached the dramatic climax of her first chapter.

"Leona gasped as she saw the upraised knife—"

And Sarah Talbot, poet, screamed.

Everyone looked at her with interest. Annabel closed her eyes and sank deeper into her chair.

"Oh, my dear," gushed Mrs. Blue. "Really, this is most gratifying, but it's just a *story*, after all."

"Not the story—it's a . . . a . . . *snake!*" cried Sarah, pointing at Wilfred, who was slithering toward the open door at top speed. Everyone looked where Sarah was pointing.

Mr. Peabody said "Oh!" and pulled his feet up on his chair. Mrs. Daphne Blue still had her manuscript in her hand. She looked down, saw Wilfred, screamed, threw the pages in the air, and jumped away from her chair. Annabel had never seen anyone that big move that fast.

Annabel's mother started closing in on Annabel, her face grim and determined. Annabel dashed forward, grabbed Wilfred, and clutched him to her chest.

"It's okay, everybody," she said weakly. "It's only Wilfred, my pet snake." Wilfred was scared by all the commotion and started to disappear under Annabel's collar.

Everyone was shouting at once. Annabel's mother was ask-

ing how did he get out, Mr. Peabody was saying, "Snakes, really!" and Mrs. Daphne Blue was across the room fanning herself with her napkin. Annabel wanted to absolutely die. Wilfred had gone and gotten them both in trouble, and all these people were yelling at him, and her mother was going to be really mad. . . . Annabel felt tears welling up in her eyes. If only she were invisible.

Then in the midst of the pandemonium, a voice said, "Wait! Quiet, everyone!"

It was Sarah Talbot. She moved toward Annabel and the crowd parted for her.

"Let me see your snake, Annabel," Sarah commanded. Annabel miserably pulled Wilfred out from under her collar and held his head up for inspection. Sarah looked him in the eye. Wilfred looked back. Everyone waited.

"Why, he's lovely!" Sarah pronounced. "He's absolutely lovely!" She smiled at Annabel. "I only screamed because I was startled. I didn't know he was a *pet* snake. I thought he was a *usurper*." Annabel didn't know what usurper meant, but she did know that the room had calmed right down.

"Yes, this is Annabel's pet snake, Wilfred," Annabel's mother explained. "He must have gotten out of his cage by accident." She looked hard at Annabel.

"Aquarium," Annabel said, and held him closer to her chest. "I don't know how he got out. I'm sorry everyone was

scared," she added in a small voice. "Wilfred's sorry too."
Wilfred hid his head under Annabel's shirt again.

"Wilfred," said Mr. Peabody. "It's a charming name. I once
had a cousin named Wilfred." He smiled at Annabel too,
although he didn't come any closer.

Mrs. Daphne Blue said, "I once made a snake the culprit
in one of my books. It was called *Murder on the Menu*." She
began to gather her pages from the floor. Annabel's mother
helped her. Annabel apologized again and said good-bye.

As she left, she heard Sarah Talbot say, "I have a fabulous
idea coming on for a poem—an ode to the snake: ancient
symbol of power and evil."

"I don't know about power, but you certainly have been
evil today, you bad boy," Annabel scolded Wilfred as she put
him back in his aquarium. "Bad, bad, bad. Was it worth it?
Are you happy? You're in complete disgrace. Don't ever do
that again." She shook her finger at him. Wilfred seemed
unconcerned as he rubbed himself against his climbing
branch.

That night, Annabel's father put two small latches on
Wilfred's lid. And Annabel had to clean up after the party
by herself—dishes and all.

8

<div align="center">~~~~~~~</div>

A Trip to the Vet

After the eventful coffee party, things quieted down for a while, to Annabel's great relief. Now that there were latches on Wilfred's aquarium, she didn't have to worry about his not being there when she got home from camp.

She fed him regularly from the wide selection of treats at Murray's Bait 'n' Tackle. He grew (she thought) another half inch. She loved to close her bedroom door and take him out of his aquarium to play. He would race across the carpet and she would almost let him get away before she swooped him up and cuddled him. Even though he wasn't furry, he was affectionate. Annabel knew that when he rubbed his head against her hair, it meant that he loved her.

Sometimes she closed her eyes and held his face next to hers. She would feel the very delicate touches of his tongue flicking against her skin like a butterfly's wings. She knew from her snake report that he was smelling her skin and identifying her. She was sure that he wasn't nearly as affectionate with other people as he was with her.

"Oh, you're kidding! He got *loose?*" shrieked Charlotte. She was finally home from her two weeks with Grandma and had called Annabel first thing. Annabel was glad she was back—she had missed Charlotte. Even though she hadn't been seeing much of her lately, it was good to know that Charlotte was always just four blocks away.

"Yep, but Dad put latches on the lid, so now he can't get out by himself anymore."

"Oh, how creepy! I can't believe he got out! What did your mother say?" asked Charlotte.

So Annabel told Charlotte the whole exciting story of how Wilfred had met the members of her mother's literary group, and how Mrs. Blue had thrown her papers all over the place. Charlotte couldn't stop laughing.

"That Wilfred is a party kind of guy, isn't he?" she asked.

"He sure is," agreed Annabel.

The next morning Annabel was dashing off to camp as usual, and she flipped up Wilfred's top to throw some mealworms in. Wilfred didn't go after them immediately, as he usually did.

I guess he isn't hungry this morning, Annabel thought as she fled for the bus.

That afternoon when she got home, she checked on Wilfred. It looked like he hadn't moved much since that morning. She took him out and put him on her bed, but he curled up instead of zooming away.

"What's the matter, boy? Are you tired?" Annabel asked him. He didn't respond, just curled up a little more. Annabel frowned and put him back in his aquarium.

At dinner that night, Annabel said, "Wilfred seems tired. Do you think Murray gave us some bad worms or something? He doesn't seem like himself."

"Maybe it's just the heat," said her mother. "It's enough to make anyone feel tired."

"But it's air conditioned in my room," Annabel answered. "I hope nothing's wrong with him."

"Oh, I'm sure he's okay, honey," said her father. "By to-morrow he'll be right as rain."

That night before going to bed Annabel examined Wilfred again. He was curled up in a corner of his aquarium, next to his pool of water. He didn't look up when Annabel reached in and stroked him gently.

The next morning Annabel jumped out of bed early to look at Wilfred. She ran out of her room and into the kitchen, where her parents were drinking coffee.

"Come quick!" she gasped. "Wilfred's really sick! He looks awful!" and she ran back down the hall to her room.

She was standing by the open aquarium when her parents came in. Wilfred was coiled loosely in his corner, completely still. Annabel could see him breathe only if she looked closely. He looked terrible. His skin had lost its healthy bright green color and was dull and grayish. Even his eyes looked cloudy—not their usual shiny black. Annabel reached in and touched him with her finger, but he didn't move.

"What's the matter with him?" she wailed.

"Well, I don't know, honey," her father began.

"Maybe he just has a cold or something," suggested her mother. "But I'll tell you what—why don't I call the people next door and see who their vet is?"

"No, let me call Charlotte. Brandy just got wormed," Annabel said. She dialed Charlotte's number, and Charlotte answered.

"Charlotte, I need the name of Brandy's vet. Wilfred's really sick," Annabel said.

"He's sick? What's wrong with him?" Charlotte asked.

"I don't know—he looks awful. I'm really worried." Annabel's voice was shaking.

"Hold on, let me get you his number. I kind of think he only does *real* pets, but you can call him. Dad takes Brandy to Dr. Zeller on Joliet Street. I hope it's nothing serious." Charlotte read his number to Annabel.

"Thanks."

"Listen, call me when you get home to tell me if he's okay," said Charlotte.

"Okay."

Annabel's mother called Dr. Zeller. He *did* see snakes too, and he fitted them in when Annabel's mother said it was an emergency.

Annabel very carefully slipped Wilfred into his traveling bag and held him gently as she and her mother drove to the vet's office.

Dr. Zeller had a nice waiting room full of panting dogs and nervous cats. Annabel sat stiffly in a chair with Wilfred cradled on her lap while her mother checked in.

Next to Annabel was an older girl holding a fancy woven wicker case. Inside, a fluffy white Persian cat with mean blue eyes was staring at Annabel. It had a pale blue satin bow tied around its neck.

"It's time for her shots," the girl explained. "She's a pure-bred Persian. What's in your bag?"

"It's my snake, Wilfred," Annabel said politely.

"A snake! Gross!" the girl said, and held her case more tightly.

Annabel stuck her tongue out at her. Who asked her, anyway?

"Annabel! It's our turn," Annabel's mother said. Annabel knew her mother had seen her stick her tongue out, but she didn't say anything.

Inside the examining room, Dr. Zeller said, "Well, what seems to be the problem here? This is a snake, I take it? Hope it's not poisonous!" He laughed. Annabel was too miserable to laugh with him. She opened Wilfred's bag and took him out. Wilfred lay in a dull gray heap on the Formica table.

"His skin is dull," Annabel said. "His eyes look bad, and he isn't eating or moving. What's wrong with him?" She had a lump in her throat.

Dr. Zeller touched Wilfred gently. Wilfred didn't move. The vet slid his finger under Wilfred's head and carefully pushed it up so he could look at Wilfred's eyes.

"How long have you had your snake?" Dr. Zeller asked.

"Almost three months," Annabel said.

"What's his name?" he asked conversationally as he pulled out his stethoscope and slid it along Wilfred's body.

"Wilfred."

Dr. Zeller smiled and held out the earpieces to Annabel so that she could listen to Wilfred's heart. Annabel heard a small whooshing sound, and very faintly, a small steady thump.

"Wilfred," said Dr. Zeller, "is going to be fine."

"He is?" Annabel said.

"Wilfred is about to molt, or shed his skin."

"Molt!" Annabel and her mother looked at each other. Annabel knew all about molting. She had even included a section on it in her end-of-the-year snake report. Her report had carefully described the symptoms of molting—dull color, listless behavior, cloudy eyes, and loss of appetite. And here she was at the *vet*. What a dumbo-head she was.

"Yep," continued Dr. Zeller cheerfully. "Snakes do it all the time, more often in summer than winter. And younger snakes do it more often than older ones. Just put him back in his cage. Does he have something to rub against in there?"

"His climbing branch." Annabel nodded sheepishly.

"Well, in a day or two, he'll start rubbing his head against the branch. And you'll notice the skin splitting around his face. He'll push it down, and then he'll sort of roll out of it, as though he were taking off a stocking. And he'll have bright new green skin again."

"And there's nothing else wrong with him?" Annabel had to make sure.

"Not a thing. He's just being a normal snake. He's probably still growing a bit. He'll do this a couple of times a year," Dr. Zeller assured her.

Annabel put Wilfred back in his bag and thanked Dr. Zeller. Her mother wrote the receptionist a check.

"I'm sorry, Mom. I guess I forgot it would happen to Wilfred," Annabel explained as they were driving home. "I hope it didn't cost too much."

"Oh, don't worry about it. I knew that snakes shed, but I

didn't think of it either. I'm relieved that he's okay," and she smiled at Annabel. Annabel was happy again. Her mother cared about Wilfred.

Back at home Annabel put Wilfred in his aquarium and left him alone. That night, Charlotte called. "Did Dr. Zeller see you?" she asked.

"Yes, he says he sees a few other snakes too. I guess they count as real pets." Annabel had not forgotten what Charlotte had said. "Wilfred's going to be fine. He's just shedding his skin."

"Shedding his skin! That's disgusting. Was that the only thing wrong?" Charlotte asked.

"Yes, and it's not even 'wrong'—for him. Snakes do it all the time. And younger snakes do it more often than older ones."

"Lovely," said Charlotte. "Well, at least he isn't dying or anything."

"No, of course he's not dying. He's going to be fine," Annabel said.

They talked some more, and Annabel made Charlotte promise to come see Wilfred's new skin in a few days.

"I'll count the minutes," Charlotte said dryly.

They hung up.

Sure enough, Annabel woke the next morning to find Wilfred rubbing his head against his branch. That afternoon his face was all green again, and by evening there was just a flat dry skin left and a brilliantly shining new Wilfred. Annabel took the old skin out, hung it next to Wilfred's growth chart, and dated it.

Wilfred was ravenous and went through twelve chirping crickets before he slowed down.

The next day Annabel bought a pale pink satin ribbon and tied it around Wilfred's neck. He looked terribly handsome.

9

Truth or Dare

Of course Wilfred dragged his nice ribbon through his water bowl and got it all dirty, so Annabel took it off. Plus it was hard to keep it up around his neck. But this morning she had washed it in the sink and was ironing it.

"Is that Wilfred's ribbon?" asked her mother.

"Yes. He's going to wear it to the party," answered Annabel.

"Does Charlotte know you're taking Wilfred to her birthday party?"

"Yes," Annabel said determinedly as she ironed the ribbon flat. She didn't tell her mother that she had had to threaten Charlotte with not coming at all before Charlotte agreed to invite Wilfred too.

"Well, for goodness sakes, *please* don't let him get loose at Charlotte's house," Annabel's mother said. "I would never hear the end of it from her mother. Okay?"

"Okay. He won't get lost. I'm taking his bag in case he gets tired," Annabel replied.

"Good idea."

So Annabel and Wilfred got dressed up for Charlotte's party.

There were already some kids at Charlotte's house when they arrived. Charlotte's parents had decorated the living room with streamers and balloons. There was a table with punch on it, and a pile of wrapped presents. Annabel added her present to the pile.

She had picked it out and wrapped it herself. It was a purple sweatshirt with beads sewn on it. Charlotte and Annabel had seen it at the shopping mall, and Charlotte had liked it.

Annabel knew everyone at the party—they were all from her class in school. The doorbell rang, and Charlotte's mother ushered more guests into the living room.

"Well, what should we do now?" asked Charlotte. "We could play Truth or Dare, or I could play my new tape."

"Hey!" said one of the boys. "Annabel, is that your snake bag?"

"Uh-huh," said Annabel, pleased that someone had noticed. "It's Wilfred. We're inseparable." Annabel opened her bag and took him out. Wilfred was a tremendous hit in his party ribbon, and everyone wanted to pet him and hold him.

"Let me see him!"

"Can I hold him?"

"Wait, everybody!" Annabel said. "You can pet him but not hold him. He doesn't like to be held by strangers." She didn't know if he did nor not, but she didn't want to take a chance.

Everyone crowded around Annabel to pet Wilfred. Finally she said, "Okay, enough for now—we don't want to wear his scales out," and casually looped him around her neck.

Charlotte, rolling her eyes, suggested playing Truth or Dare again. But when it was Charlotte's turn and she chose "dare," Barry Johnson (whom her mother had *made* her invite) dared her to—

"Kiss Wilfred! Kiss— Are you crazy?" Charlotte cried. Annabel couldn't help smiling, and playfully held Wilfred's head up.

Charlotte looked horrified. She turned to stare at Annabel. Annabel could tell that even the thought of kissing Wilfred was enough to turn Charlotte's stomach. Suddenly Annabel felt a pang of guilt. Here she was, Charlotte's best friend, supposedly, and she was helping stinky Barry Johnson pick on her at her own birthday party.

Charlotte's face hardened, and she glared at Annabel and put her hands on her hips. She approached the subject in question. Annabel's eyes widened as Charlotte rooted her feet firmly on the ground, clamped her hand around Wilfred's skinny green neck, screwed her eyes shut, and planted a big, wet, smackeroo right between Wilfred's eyes.

She stepped back and looked around. No one was laughing anymore. They were standing around uncomfortably, looking at each other with surprised expressions.

"There!" Charlotte said to them. "I did it. Are you happy?" No one said anything. Barry Johnson looked at his feet. Annabel held Wilfred down by her side. She wished she hadn't brought him.

"And how about you, Miss Annabel Bentley, my so-called best friend? Are *you* glad you—" Charlotte paused, her lip quivering. Her eyes filled with embarrassed tears.

"Oh, forget it!" Charlotte cried, and ran upstairs to her room.

Everyone was silent. Charlotte's mother came out from the kitchen to see what was happening.

Annabel felt terrible. She unhooked Wilfred from around her neck and quietly put him in his bag.

"I have to go talk to Charlotte," she said. Charlotte's mother nodded, then started gathering the other kids for some party games.

When Annabel got to Charlotte's room, Charlotte was sitting on her bed blowing her nose into a Kleenex. Annabel closed the door behind her.

"Charlotte," she began. Charlotte looked up.

"What do *you* want?" she asked, and wiped her eyes.

"I want to apologize," Annabel said. "I was stupid to make you let me bring Wilfred. If it were my party, I'd want to be getting all the attention." Apologizing was hard.

Charlotte sniffled.

"I didn't bring Brandy to your stupid old birthday party," she said.

"I know, I know. I'm sorry," said Annabel.

"It's *my* birthday. I should get to say who comes or not."

"I know," repeated Annabel. Geez, when was this going to end? Annabel was sorry, enough was enough.

"Ever since you got that dumb snake I hardly ever see you anymore. We used to play together all the time. Now it's just Wilfred this and Wilfred that. I'm sick of Wilfred!" Charlotte burst into tears all over again.

"Ohhh," Annabel said. She sat down next to Charlotte and patted her shoulder. "Oh, Charlotte, I didn't know you thought that. It's just—well, I was so happy to finally have a pet of my own. You always had Brandy to play with, and I would go home and have no pet and be so jealous."

"Jealous of Brandy?" Charlotte asked, wiping her eyes.

"Uh-huh. Wilfred is the only pet I can have because my dad is allergic to everything with fur," explained Annabel.

"Oh," said Charlotte. "Oh."

"Listen, I would take Wilfred home now if I could—but I can't. Can I leave him in his bag in here while we go back to the party? That is, if you want me to stay. I hope you're still my best friend, Charlotte. I'd like to stay," Annabel said uncertainly.

She thought if she were Charlotte, she might not want her to stay.

Charlotte looked up. "Yes, you can stay. Am I really still your best friend?" she asked.

"Of course you are," said Annabel. "It's just that Wilfred's my *pet*; he lives with me. But *you're* who I *talk* to."

Charlotte smiled, then asked, "Won't Wilfred mind being cooped up in his bag?"

"No, he doesn't mind. He's used to it. He just goes to sleep. Want to see?" Annabel asked.

"Well, okay."

Annabel opened the drawstring and pulled Wilfred out a little. He was calm, but didn't look bored or anything. Annabel held her breath while Charlotte slowly reached out a finger to stroke Wilfred's side. Wilfred moved toward Charlotte, and she petted him softly.

"He likes you!" said Annabel. "He doesn't let just anyone touch him."

"He doesn't?" asked Charlotte. She smiled. "He isn't slimy at all. He's sort of smooth."

The two girls sat there happily, smiling and petting Wilfred, who was basking in the attention.

"He's kind of nice," said Charlotte. "Do you really think he likes me?"

"Absolutely!" said Annabel.

Charlotte and Annabel rejoined the party while Wilfred napped in his bag in Charlotte's room. There was white cake with vanilla icing, and games to play, which were sort of babyish but still fun.

It turned into a good party, and Annabel didn't take Wilfred out again. Soon they forgot that he was even there. Annabel stayed late, helping Charlotte pick up wrapping paper and having seconds of cake and ice cream.

They put Charlotte's presents in her room. Her big present from her parents had been a fashion doll and her beachhouse set.

"Look at this," Charlotte whispered. "I don't like it. I never play with stuff like this. Where did they get this idea from?"

Annabel shrugged. Who knew where parents got their ideas?

"What would you rather have?" Annabel whispered back. Charlotte glanced at Wilfred's bag lying on her bed.

"I think," she said, "well, you know—I love Brandy a lot and all, but he really belongs to my parents. I think I'd like to have a pet of my very own."

Annabel giggled. "Hmmm," she said.

"Guess who I saw today," said Annabel's mother as she came in with the groceries a few days later.

Annabel and Michael looked up. They were reading the funnies on the floor.

"I saw Charlotte and her mother in the parking lot outside Petworld." She put her bags down on the kitchen counter. "A man was helping them load a large aquarium into the back of their station wagon." She took off her sunglasses and paused for dramatic effect. "Charlotte was holding a cardboard box with air holes punched in it that said 'Live Iguana.' "